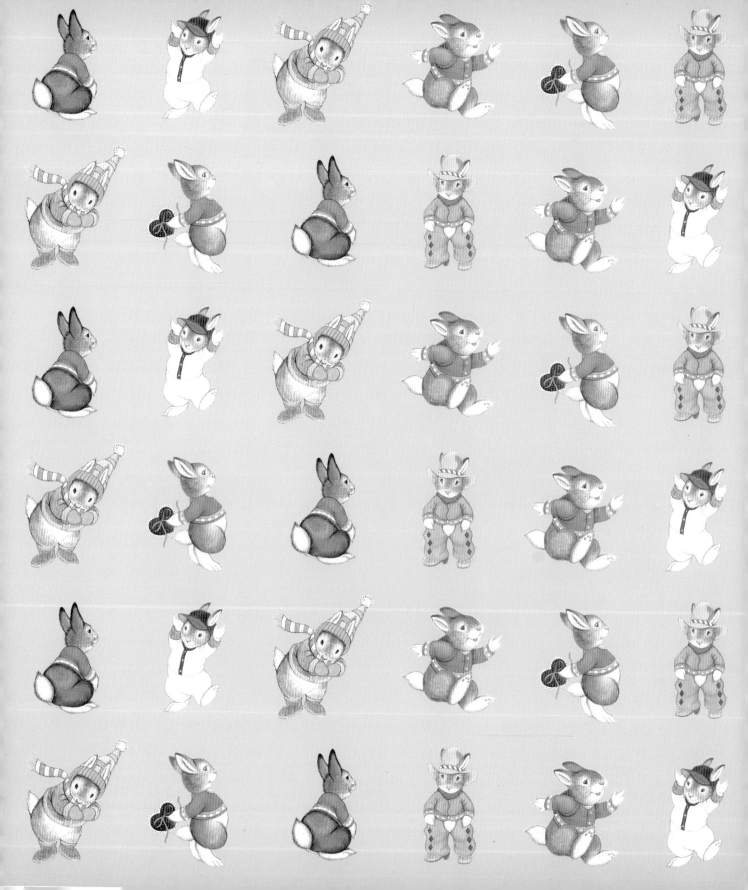

波波 唸翻天系列 8

聖誕快樂，波波！

Justine Korman 著

Lucinda McQueen 繪

何信彰 譯

三民書局

For all the everyday Santas
finding ways to give their love.
—J.K.

獻給所有平凡的聖誕老人
感謝他們努力不懈地散播愛心
— J.K.

Merry Christmas to Marissa and Benjamin.
Lots of love,
— Lucy

聖誕節快樂，瑪麗莎和班傑明
好愛你們
— 露西

Christmas was coming! Everyone at Easter Bunny Elementary School was full of good **cheer**—except Hopper. The grumpy bunny couldn't have felt grumpier.

聖誕節就快到了！復活節兔寶寶小學裡的每一個人都滿心歡喜——只有波波例外，這隻愛發牢騷的兔子不耐煩到了極點。

Hopper was tired of shopping. His feet hurt. And after buying **presents** for everyone else, he couldn't **afford** the foot **massager** he wanted for himself.

"No one ever gets me what I really want," Hopper grumbled. "It's always just boring sweaters and itchy socks."

波波買東西已經買到煩了，他的兩隻腳痠痛得不得了，而且幫其他人買了禮物之後，他就沒有錢買自己想要的腳底按摩器了。

「從來沒有人送給我我真正想要的東西，」波波嘀咕著：「每次都一成不變，送的不是毛衣，就是穿了以後腳會發癢的襪子。」

And if anybunny else asked him where his holiday **spirit** was, Hopper was going to scream!

要是這時還有哪個不識相的兔寶寶問他為什麼聖誕節還這樣悶悶不樂，他可就真的要發飆了！

Suddenly, Lilac **burst into** the room. The pretty music teacher was excited.

"Guess who's going to be Mrs. Claus at the Bunnyburg Mall?" she said. "Me! And they still need someone to be Santa. But if they don't find somebunny soon, the mall manager will **call off** the **performance**."

突然間，漂亮的丁香老師很興奮地衝進教室。
「你猜今年兔兔堡購物城裡的聖誕老婆婆是誰？」她跟波波說：「是我耶！他們還要找一個聖誕老公公，不過要是他們沒有盡快找到的話，購物城的經理就要把這項表演取消了。」

Hopper could tell where this was going. And he didn't like it. "You want *me* to be **Santa Claus** for a bunch of whining bunnies in a crowded mall?" he asked.

波波能了解丁香老師說的狀況，不過他並不喜歡這份差事，「你要我到人擠人的購物城裡當聖誕老公公？然後還得應付一大群鬼叫鬼叫的兔寶寶嗎？」他問。

Lilac smiled. And Hopper's heart **melted** as his sore feet throbbed.
He could never say no to Lilac.

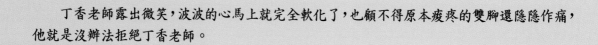
丁香老師露出微笑，波波的心馬上就完全軟化了，也顧不得原本疲疼的雙腳還隱隱作痛，
他就是沒辦法拒絕丁香老師。

"We **rehearse** at eight A.M. and open at nine on Christmas Eve. I'll take you to the manager's office. He has your Santa **suit** there. Thank you so much, Hopper," Lilac said sweetly.

「我們在聖誕節前一天的上午八點彩排，九點開始表演，我會帶你去經理的辦公室，他替你準備了聖誕老人的衣服。真是太謝謝你了，波波。」丁香老師親切地說。

On Christmas Eve, the grumpy bunny **wriggled** into the itchy Santa **costume**. Lilac made a lovely Mrs. Claus. Together, they followed the busy mall manager as he quickly told them what to do.

聖誕節的前一天，波波硬是擠進了那件穿了會讓人發癢的聖誕老人服，丁香老師也打扮成一位很可愛的聖誕老婆婆，然後忙碌的經理很快地跟他們說明應該要怎麼做，他們倆也依樣畫葫蘆。

"Basically, you sit the bunnies on your **lap**, one at a time, listen to what they want for Christmas, say 'ho-ho-ho,' and send them on their way," the manager said. "Any questions?"

Hopper **shook** his head.

「基本上，你要讓兔寶寶們坐在你的腿上，一次一隻就好，然後認真聽他們聖誕節想要什麼東西，還要發出『呵—呵—呵』的笑聲，最後再送他們離開。」經理解釋完以後問他：「有什麼問題嗎？」

波波搖搖頭。

They had a few minutes left before the mall opened. Lilac used the time to **recall** what Santa had **meant** to her when she was young.

購物城還要再過幾分鐘後才會開門，丁香老師趁著這段空檔，回想小時候聖誕老公公對她的意義。

"All year I tried so hard to be good. I did my homework and **chores**, and **practiced** the piano. It often seemed as if no one noticed —except Santa."

「一整年我都很努力做個乖小孩，認真做功課，也幫忙做家事，還練習彈鋼琴，好像都沒有人注意到我這麼認真——除了聖誕老公公以外。」

"Every Christmas season I waited and hoped. On that **magic** day, Santa would always bring something wonderful," Lilac marveled. "I loved to **picture** him in his bright red suit, so merry and kind."

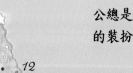

「每年到了聖誕假期，我都會耐心地等，內心充滿期待，到了神奇的那一天，聖誕老公公總是會帶來很棒的禮物，」丁香老師讚嘆地說：「我很喜歡想像聖誕老公公身穿大紅色衣服的裝扮，很快樂也很慈祥。」

Suddenly, Hopper felt proud of his itchy costume.
He was **determined** to be the best Santa he could be!

這時候，波波忽然對他這身讓人發癢的聖誕老人裝感到自豪，他下定決心要盡全力做個最棒的聖誕老公公！

各個入口都打開了，最早到的兔寶寶們一湧而上，衝向波波。

The doors opened, and the first arrivals came rushing up to Hopper.
The little bunnies **squealed** with **delight** at the sight of him.
Hopper ho-ho-ho'd. This wasn't so bad. In fact, it was fun!

小兔寶寶一看到他，都高興得發出尖叫聲，波波呵呵呵地大笑，這種感覺還不壞嘛，老實說，還蠻有趣的哩！

這隻原本愛抱怨的兔子不再有一肚子的牢騷，他也感染了聖誕節的快樂氣氛！

The grumpy bunny wasn't grumpy anymore. He had the Christmas spirit! He felt full of love and joy!

整個人洋溢著愛和喜樂！

But as the hours went by, Hopper's lap got tired. His head began to **ache**. He found out that being Santa isn't all cookies and milk.

不過幾個小時過去之後，波波的腿變痠，頭也痛了起來，他發現當聖誕老公公可不是件輕鬆的事。

One bunny **tugged** at Hopper's **beard** and cried, "You're not the real Santa Claus!"

有一隻兔寶寶用力扯波波的鬍子，然後大叫著說：「你不是真的聖誕老公公嘛！」

Some of the little bunnies were **scared**! They screamed in
Hopper's ears.

另外有一些小兔寶寶被嚇壞了！當著波波的面大哭大鬧。

Other bunnies couldn't decide
what to ask for. Hopper tried to be
patient.

還有一些兔寶寶沒辦法決定到底要跟聖誕老公公要什麼禮物，波波也盡量保持耐性。

"Your *ho-ho-ho* is **lame**!" said one visitor. Another **complained**,
"Last year's Santa was better." Hopper sighed.

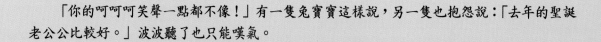

「你的呵呵呵笑聲一點都不像！」有一隻兔寶寶這樣說，另一隻也抱怨說：「去年的聖誕老公公比較好。」波波聽了也只能嘆氣。

Some bunnies were **rowdy**, like the young twins who wanted a trampoline.

有些兔寶寶很愛無理取鬧，像有一對幼小的雙胞胎就吵著要彈簧墊。

Other bunnies were downright **naughty**. When Hopper tried to stop an **argument**, he accidentally got **punched** in the nose!

"Ow-ow-ow!" Santa Hopper wailed.

"That's 'ho-ho-ho,'" the manager corrected.

其他的兔寶寶也頑皮得很，波波本來想要安撫兩隻吵架的兔寶寶，反而不小心給一拳打中鼻子！

「噢—噢—噢！」聖誕老人波波痛得大叫。

「應該是『呵—呵—呵』才對，」經理糾正他。

Through it all, Hopper tried to stay true to Lilac's **image** of Santa. He made sure his *ho-ho-ho*'s were merry. And he had a kind word for everybunny, even the one who **sneezed** on his beard.

從頭到尾,波波都很努力,希望表現得跟丁香老師心目中的聖誕老公公一樣好,他每一次「呵—呵—呵」的笑聲都是發自內心的快樂。而且他對每一隻兔寶寶都和顏悅色,就連有一隻兔寶寶把噴嚏打到他臉上,他還是面不改色。

Finally, the long day was over. Hopper **dragged** himself home on his weary feet. As he neared his **cozy** little house, he realized he was still wearing the Santa suit.

"Oh, **bah humbug!**" he griped. "I'll have to take it back to the mall the day after Christmas."

好不容易，漫長的一天終於結束了，波波拖著疲倦的腳步回家，就在他快要回到自己的溫馨小屋時，才發現自己身上還穿著聖誕老公公的服裝。

「哼，真討厭！」他又發起牢騷：「聖誕節隔天，我還得把衣服拿去還給購物城呢。」

Just then, Hopper noticed a brightly **wrapped package** on his doorstep. What could it be?

就在那時候，波波注意到在門口的階梯上，有一個包裝得很鮮艷的包裹，會是什麼東西呢？

He read the gift **tag**: To SANTA FRON SANTA. Hopper looked up. For just a moment, he thought he saw a **sleigh** in the sky! But when he **rubbed** his tired eyes, the vision was gone.

Hopper shook his head. *Maybe the package is from Lilac,* he thought.

他唸著禮物上的標籤:「聖誕老人送給聖誕老人的禮物。」波波抬頭一看,在那一瞬間,
他覺得自己看到天空中有一輛雪橇!不過當他再揉一揉疲勞的眼睛,就什麼也沒有了。
波波搖了搖頭,心想這個包裹也許是丁香老師送的。

Hopper hurried into the house and **tore** open the box. Inside, he found...a foot massager! How wonderful! For once, the grumpy bunny had **received** exactly what he wanted.

But it wasn't really the foot machine that made Hopper so happy. It was the feeling that Lilac had **described**. Someone had noticed how hard he was trying and had made a special effort to bring him the perfect **reward**.

波波趕緊衝到屋子裡，拆開盒子，發現裡頭裝的原來是……一臺腳底按摩器！真是太棒了！終於有這麼一次，波波收到了他真正想要的禮物。

不過讓波波這麼開心的，並不是這臺腳底按摩器，而是丁香老師之前形容的那種感覺，因為有人注意到他的努力，所以也特別用心送給他這麼好的禮物作為回報。

Hopper put his tired feet inside the massager and sighed happily. Now he was **looking forward to** Christmas. He couldn't wait to give gifts to all the bunnies he loved. Just the thought of it made his **belly** shake with a genuine *ho-ho-ho!*

*You don't need a beard or eight tiny **reindeer***
to spread lots of joy and Christmas cheer:
Just find the love that's deep inside,
and you'll give someone a sweet surprise!

波波把疲痛的雙腳放到按摩器裡面,發出了滿足的長嘆聲,現在的他很期待聖誕節的來臨,他已經等不及要把禮物分送給所有他喜歡的兔寶寶了,想到這裡,他呵呵呵地笑著,肚子也隨著笑聲抖動,而這次波波的笑聲終於像聖誕老公公的笑聲了!

就算鬍子、馴鹿都沒著落,聖誕節還是能歡喜快樂過;
只要發掘內心深處的愛意,就能帶給別人甜蜜的驚喜。

costume [`kɑstjum] 名 戲服
cozy [`kozɪ] 形 舒適的

ache [ek] 動 痛
afford [`əford] 動 負擔得起
argument [`ɑrgjəmənt] 名 爭論

delight [dɪ`laɪt] 名 高興
describe [dɪ`skraɪb] 動 形容
determine [dɪ`tɝmɪn] 動 決定
drag [dræg] 動 緩慢地前進

bah [bɑ] 感 哼（表示嫌惡的感嘆詞）
beard [bɪrd] 名 鬍子
belly [`bɛlɪ] 名 肚子
burst into 衝進…

humbug [`hʌm,bʌg] 名 騙子

call off 取消
cheer [tʃɪr] 名 心情
chore [tʃɔr] 名 家事
complain [kəm`plen] 動 抱怨

image [`ɪmɪdʒ] 名 （心中描繪的）形象

performance [pɚˋfɔrməns] 名 演出

picture [ˋpɪktʃɚ] 動 想像

practice [ˋpræktɪs] 動 練習

present [ˋprɛzn̩t] 名 禮物

punch [pʌntʃ] 動 用拳頭猛擊

L

lame [lem] 形 缺少說服力的

lap [læp] 名 人坐下時膝部和大腿部分

look forward to 期待

M

magic [ˋmædʒɪk] 形 神奇的

massager [məˋsɑʒɚ] 名 按摩器

mean [min] 動 有…意義

melt [mɛlt] 動 溶化

N

naughty [ˋnɔtɪ] 形 沒有禮貌的

P

package [ˋpækɪdʒ] 名 包裹

patient [ˋpeʃənt] 形 有耐性的

R

recall [rɪˋkɔl] 動 回想

receive [rɪˋsiv] 動 收到

rehearse [rɪˋhɝs] 動 排演

reindeer [ˋren‚dɪr] 名 馴鹿

reward [rɪˋwɔrd] 名 獎勵

rowdy [ˋraʊdɪ] 形 吵鬧的

rub [rʌb] 動 摩擦

S

Santa Claus 名 聖誕老人

scare [skɛr] 動 使驚嚇

shake [ʃek] 動 搖動

sleigh [sle] 名 雪橇

sneeze [sniz] 動 打噴嚏

spirit [ˋspɪrɪt] 名 精神

squeal [skwil] 動 發出尖銳的歡呼聲

suit [sut] 名（為特定目的所準備的）服裝

tag [tæg] 名 標籤

tear [tɛr] 動 撕破

tug [tʌg] 動 用力拉

wrap [ræp] 動 包裝

wriggle [`rɪgl̩] 動 掙扎

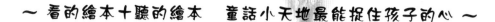

~ 看的繪本＋聽的繪本　童話小天地最能捉住孩子的心 ~

為孩子寫～彩色的夢

🌀 兒童文學叢書

·童話小天地·

● **奇妙的紫貝殼** /附CD
簡 宛·文　朱美靜·圖

● **奇奇的磁鐵鞋** /附CD
林黛嫚·文　黃子瑄·圖

● **九重葛笑了** /附CD
陳 冷·文　吳佩蓁·圖

● **智慧市的糊塗市民** /附CD
劉靜娟·文　邰欣／倪靖·圖

● **銀毛與斑斑** /附CD
李民安·文　廖健宏·圖

● **丁伶郎** /附CD
潘人木·文
鄭凱軍／羅小紅·圖

● **屋頂上的祕密** /附CD
劉靜娟·文　郝洛玟·圖

● **石頭不見了** /附CD
李民安·文　翔 子·圖
榮獲行政院新聞局
第五屆圖畫故事類小太陽獎

嗨～猜猜爸爸進裡的是哪一本？爸爸媽媽甜蜜的說故事時間就要開始囉！

國家圖書館出版品預行編目資料

聖誕快樂，波波！ / Justine Korman著;Lucinda Mc-
Queen繪;何信彰譯.－－初版一刷.－－臺北市；三
民，民91
　　面;公分－－(探索英文叢書.波波唸翻天系列;8)
中英對照
ISBN 957-14-3439-6　(一套；平裝)

1.英國語言—讀本

805.18

網路書店位址：http://www.sanmin.com.tw

ⓒ　聖誕快樂，波波！

著作人　Justine Korman
繪圖者　Lucinda McQueen
譯　者　何信彰
發行人　劉振強
著作財　三民書局股份有限公司
產權人　臺北市復興北路三八六號
發行所　三民書局股份有限公司
　　　　地址／臺北市復興北路三八六號
　　　　電話／二五○○六六○○
　　　　郵撥／○○○九九九八——五號
印刷所　三民書局股份有限公司
門市部　復北店／臺北市復興北路三八六號
　　　　重南店／臺北市重慶南路一段六十一號
初版一刷　中華民國九十一年一月
編　號　S 85603
定　價　新臺幣壹佰捌拾元整
行政院新聞局登記證局版臺業字第○二○○號

ISBN　957-14-3579-1　(平裝)

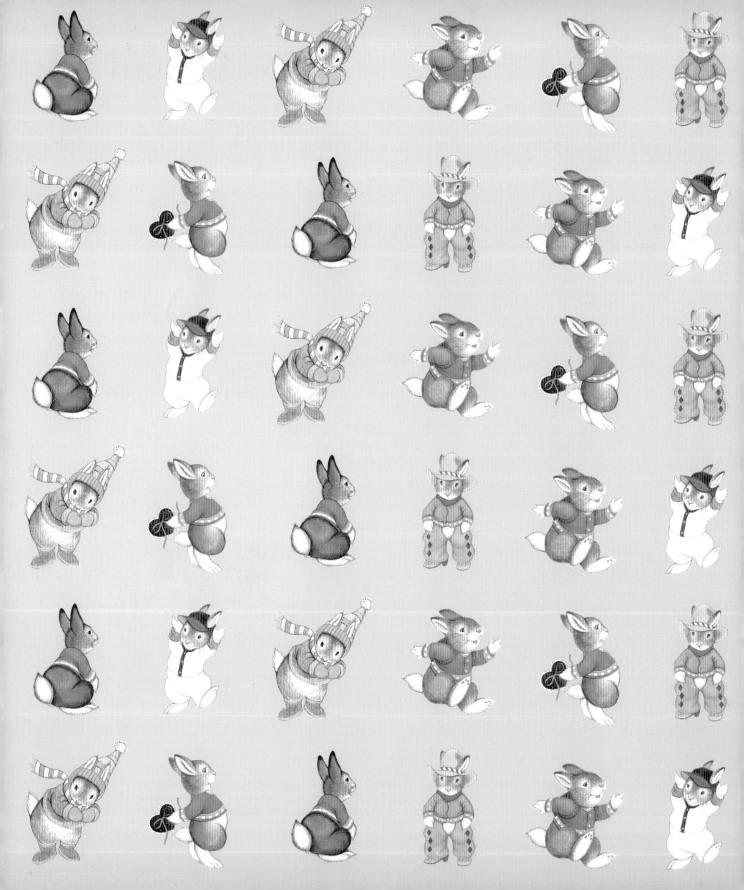